The Adventures of

Lily

and the Little Lost Doggie

Hubble & Hattie

Written and illustrated by **Laura Hamilton**

The Hubble & Hattie imprint was launched in 2009, and is named in memory of two very special Westie sisters owned by Veloce's proprietors. Since the first book, many more have been added, all with the same objective: to be of real benefit to the species they cover; at the same time promoting compassion, understanding and respect between all animals (including human ones!)

In 2017, the first Hubble & Hattie Kids! book – *Worzel says hello! Will you be my friend?* – was published, and has subsequently been joined by many more.

Our new range of books for kids will champion the same values and standards that we've always held dear, but to the adults of the future. Children will love reading, or having these beautifully illustrated, carefully crafted publications read to them, absorbing valuable life lessons whilst being highly entertained. We've more great books already in the pipeline so remember to check out our website for details.

Also from Hubble & Hattie Kids!

Worzel says hello! Will you be my friend? (by Catherine Pickles, illustrated by Chantal Bourgonje)

Worzel goes for a walk! Will you come too? (by Catherine Pickles, illustrated by Chantal Bourgonje)

The Lucky, Lucky Leaf – A Horace and Nim Story (by Chantal Bourgonje and David Hoskins, illustrated by Chantal Bourgonje)

Positive thinking for Piglets – A Horace and Nim Story (by Chantal Bourgonje and David Hoskins, illustrated by Chantal Bourgonje)

Fierce Grey Mouse (written and illustrated by Chantal Bourgonje)

The Wandering Wildebeest (by Martin Coleman, illustrated by Tim Slater)

Indigo Warriors (by Catherine James)

The Little House that didn't have a home (by Neil Sullivan, illustrated by Steven Burke)

My Grandad can draw anything – BUT he can't draw hands! (by Neil Sullivan, illustrated by Steven Burke)

www.hubbleandhattie.com

First published in August 2019 by Veloce Publishing Limited, Veloce House, Parkway Farm Business Park, Middle Farm Way, Poundbury, Dorchester DT1 3AR, England. Tel +44 (0)1305 260068 / Fax 01305 250479 / e-mail info@veloce.co.uk / web www.veloce.co.uk or www.velocebooks.com.
ISBN: 978-1-787114-18-0; UPC: 6-36847-01418-6.

The Adventures of Lily

and the Little Lost Doggie

Written and illustrated by **Laura Hamilton**

Dedication

In memory of Jim, my wonderful husband, my soul mate.
I chose the Dragon Rapide, the Boeing 737 and the Piper
Warrior as illustrations for Chapters 6 and 7, because these
three were among the many airplanes that were very special
to him. Also, he would certainly have understood Jack's
enthusiasm for model airplanes.

In memory of my amazing mother, Margaret, who
encouraged me as I illustrated my published children's
stories in Canada. That experience prepared me to illustrate
this book. She would have been thrilled with my illustrations
here.

Contents

Chapter 1

The Amazing Adventures Begin!

Lily is a Golden Retriever. Her amazing adventures began the minute she and her human mummy, Anne Fairchild, left their house for school.

Walking along the path by their hedge, Lily suddenly pulled her lead tight. She turned and sniffed. Something smelled different. Straight away, she followed her nose under the hedge.

"What are you doing?" Anne asked, astonished.

But Lily wasn't listening to Anne. She was listening to what Anne couldn't hear: a little voice, sobbing.

Lily dived into the hedge. When she backed out, she held something fluffy in her mouth.

"What's this?" Anne asked, gently taking it. She brushed away leaves and twigs and dirt. "It's a toy doggie," she said, straightening its ears. "Why on earth was it under the hedge?"

Lily wondered, too. She asked the little toy doggie, but he only whimpered, which was no answer at all.

"He must be lost," Anne said. She held him tenderly. "You're lucky Lily found you, little doggie. No one would see you under the hedge. I know what to do. We have to hurry, Lily, or we'll be late for school."

Lily didn't want to be late. School was fun. Children read books to her and gave her treats and fussed her.

Anne dashed into their house with the little lost doggie. He let his arms and legs bounce up and down. It felt good not to be squashed in the hedge any more.

Lily trotted behind Anne to see what she was doing. Pilot, Lily's dog mummy, appeared. She'd been watching them from the front window.

"What's happening?" Pilot asked.

"I found a little lost doggie. Mummy's going to help him," Lily said.

Anne untangled a purple ribbon from a kitchen drawer and rushed back outside with Lily. She tied the lost doggie to the lamppost opposite their front window.

"You look cute with that bow," she said. "Are you comfy under the ribbon?"

He'd never been asked if he was comfy. He couldn't think what to say.

"Your owner should see you here." Anne nodded. "They may even find you before we get home. Now, let's go, Lily, or we'll be late!"

Lily looked up at the little lost doggie.

7

As she trotted off to school with Anne, she kept glancing back at him until they turned the corner. He watched them rush away, and he was alone again.

Anne and Lily got to school in time. Today, a little boy read from *Simon Super-Paws: 009, Secret Agent* to Lily. Though Simon was a cat, she still liked hearing about his adventures.

But not today. Today, she couldn't focus. Her thoughts wandered back to the doggie. Was he okay? Had his owner come? Was he still on the lamppost?

When Anne and Lily were nearly home, they saw that he was exactly where they'd left him. Lily wondered how he'd got lost. And she worried that he was scared, all alone on the lamppost.

"You poor little lost doggie," said Anne. "No sign of your owner yet. Well, there's always more than one way to solve a problem. I have another idea to help you get found."

She used her phone to take a photo of the doggie, then went inside with Lily.

Pilot greeted them. She wondered what was going on.

Anne opened her laptop. Lily and Pilot sat beside her to read as she typed: 'Found toy waiting for owner on no. 2 lamppost, of Woodland Brook Walk, Haven.'

Anne attached the doggie's photo, then clicked SEND.

"Done," she said. "I've put the doggie on Lost It? Find It! Anyone who's lost something can find it there. The doggie's owner will be able to find him now."

All afternoon the little lost doggie watched for his owner from the lamppost. All afternoon Anne went back and forth to her laptop, checking Lost It? Find It! All afternoon Lily and Pilot watched the doggie from the window.

"Little doggie," said Lily. "This is Pilot, my dog mummy."

"Hi, little doggie," said Pilot. "Why were you under the hedge?"

He looked at them and shook his head. He said ever so softly, "I can't think."

Lily and Pilot were sad for him. They stayed at the window to keep him company.

Behind them, Anne sighed. "I've had no replies to Lost It? Find It! Come away from the window now, girls. It's dark."

"Goodnight, little doggie," Lily whispered as Anne drew the curtains.

The little lost doggie was left to spend the night alone on the lamppost. Lily had to wait until morning to talk to him again.

But what if he wasn't there? She slumped, her head on her paws, peering at the closed curtains. She wasn't sure she wanted the doggie to go. But if he was still there, that meant his owner hadn't come for him. Lily whimpered, imagining how awful she'd feel if Anne didn't come back for her.

If no one ever came for the little lost doggie, what would happen to him then?

Chapter 2

Watching and Waiting

The first thing Lily did when she woke up the next morning was see if the doggie was still on the lamppost. She tugged on the living room curtains and her tail wagged. He was still there!

Upstairs, Anne opened her bedroom curtains and saw he hadn't been taken away overnight.

"He's sleeping," Anne said when she found Lily watching him. "A tired little doggie. Looks like he stayed safe last night. We can check on him on our walk."

Anne slipped harnesses onto Lily and Pilot, and they went on their before-breakfast walk. Passing the lamppost, Lily and Pilot could hear the doggie softly snoring. On the way home, they stopped so Anne could check he was comfy. He didn't even wake up.

It was Pilot's day to go to school and listen to the children read. After breakfast, Anne told Lily, "We're not coming home straight from school. I have lots of signs to put up about our little lost doggie."

Lily watched them leave. Then she looked out the window at the doggie. She noticed him wiggle a little, and tilted her head to one side. He wiggled a little more, and her tail thumped softly against the carpet. He was waking up.

"Hi," she called to him. "How do you feel?"

He whispered in a shy little voice, "I'm not sure." He blinked in the sunshine and stretched as much as the ribbon would let him.

"Did you have a good sleep?" Lily asked hopefully.

"Oh, no!" He yawned, politely putting both paws in front of his mouth. "I didn't fall asleep until the sun came up. There were so many curious animals keeping me awake. Some were nice, like the doe and her new baby. And the cat. She purred and rubbed against the lamppost. And the hedgehog who snuffled around with her babies. But the foxes were scary. They sneaked around, then vanished into shadows. The bats startled me. They zoomed by so close. The owls were spooky. All night long they hooted, 'Whoooo are you?' But I couldn't tell them," he whispered wearily. "I don't know who I am."

"We don't know either," said Lily. "Can you tell me your name?"

"I don't think I have a name," he told her. He let his head hang down.

"Everyone needs a name," said Lily brightly. "Maybe we should find you one!"

The little doggie lifted his head in interest.

"What about 'Doggie'?" Lily asked. "Could we call you that for now?"

For the first time, Doggie smiled. "Oh, yes, please! I'd like to be a doggie. Being called Doggie will make me feel like a doggie!"

He wriggled with happiness. But it didn't last long. He remembered why he was still on the lamppost. "No one wants me."

"That's not true," Lily assured him. "We want you to be happy back with your owner. That's who Mummy's trying to find. She's out with Pilot, putting up lots of signs about you for your owner to see. Yesterday, she put a notice about you on Lost It? Find It! Maybe you should put your own notice up?"

Doggie wondered what Lost It? Find It! was. He was about to ask Lily but she had scampered away. When she came back, she was pushing Anne's footstool up under the window. Anne's laptop was on it.

"Think what you want to write." Lily panted with excitement as she opened the laptop.

"I've never had a think," Doggie said.

"My head is just full of fluff."

"Not everyone can be good at thinks," Lily said to comfort him. "Some are good at doings."

"I'm not sure I'm good at doings, either," he said sadly.

"Everyone's good at something," Lily soothed. "Even if it's good at just being." Her tail started wagging. "Don't worry. I'll help you."

Chapter 3

"Girls! Where's Doggie?"

Anne had tied Doggie to the lamppost for his owner to find him. She had put a notice about him on Lost It? Find It! Now, she was out putting up signs about him.

The problem was that Doggie's owner still hadn't come for him. Lily remembered how Anne would often say, "There's always more than one way to solve a problem." And so Lily had thought of another way to solve the problem. Lily and Doggie were going to write Doggie's own post for Lost It? Find It!

"Now, what shall we write?" Lily asked Doggie. "Three thinks should be enough."

Three thinks? Doggie didn't have even one think in his head. Only fluff. How could he have three thinks? He wriggled nervously on the lamppost and said nothing.

"Doggie? I have Lost It? Find It! ready," Lily reminded

him. But Doggie just looked at the ground. Lily started the post for him anyway. "Let's make the first think about where you are."

Lily's paws flew over the laptop's keyboard as she quickly typed the first think.

Then she asked, "Shall we make your second think about getting an ID? That way, you'll always know who you are."

"Okay," Doggie agreed. He didn't know what IDs were, but Lily made them sound important.

Lily's paws flew across the keyboard again.

"Your third think should be about microchips," Lily told him.

"Oh," Doggie said, "they sound yummy."

"Microchips aren't yummy," Lily explained. "They're magical! You can't see them, but they can talk. My microchip can tell someone how to get me back to Mummy if I get lost."

Lily's paws flew over the keyboard once more. Her nails went clickety, clackety, clickety, clackety.

"That's three thinks!" Lily beamed. She read it to Doggie:

Lily rescued me from under a hedge, and her mummy tied me to a lamppost so you could see me. I've been watching for you since yesterday but you haven't come. I'm on lamppost number 2,

Woodland Brook Walk, Haven. Lily says all doggies should have a microchip and a collar with ID to help them get home if they get lost. When you find me, can we please get them for me? From Doggie. (That's what Lily calls me.)

Lily finished reading. "I added 'please' because you're so polite. Does that sound okay?"

Doggie replied, "Oh, yes, it sounds lovely!"

Lily clicked SEND. Doggie's notice zoomed away.

Just before Anne took Lily and Pilot for their last walk of the day, she checked Lost It? Find It!

Anne laughed. "Oh, wow! Lots of replies!" She quickly read them all. "Let's go tell the little doggie!"

Right away, they went out to the lamppost.

Making sure the purple ribbon was still okay, Anne smiled at Doggie. "There's lots of interest in you on Lost It? Find It! Everyone is calling you Doggie, so I will, too. They all want to buy you a collar with an ID and get you a microchip. With so many replies, you won't be on the lamppost long."

Feeling happy for Doggie, Anne, Lily and Pilot went off for their walk.

Coming home, Anne saw Doggie's lamppost. But Doggie wasn't on it.

"Girls!" Anne cried. "Where's Doggie?"

Had his owner finally seen a notice and come for him?

What Anne saw next made her heart sink: Doggie was on the grass, a little way from the lamppost. Something terrible must have happened.

"Doggie!" she exclaimed.

She gently picked him up. "Poor Doggie. Are you okay?"

Doggie felt damp, and Anne couldn't think why. It hadn't been raining. Doggie had been crying, and his tears had soaked into his fur.

It was when Anne looked up that she became really puzzled.

"How can your ribbon still be tied on the lamppost when you aren't?" she asked him. "You couldn't have slipped out. And how did you end up all the way over here on the grass?"

Now, Anne had two mysteries to solve.

Chapter 4

Oh No! Mysteries Solved

Doggie had been on the lamppost when Anne, Lily and Pilot had left for their walk, so Anne knew he hadn't been on the ground for very long.

She brushed the grass off him, then tied him back onto the lamppost with the purple ribbon, just like before.

But two mysteries still puzzled her. How had Doggie ended up so far from the lamppost? And how had the ribbon been left behind?

Doggie couldn't tell her. She had to find out herself.

Luckily, Anne had CCTV. Her camera had recorded everything. Inside, as she watched the clip on her mobile, she told the girls, "Mysteries solved ..."

It was so hard for her to believe. Three boys had come down the street. Two older boys were kicking a football. One noticed Doggie and pointed at him, then said something to the youngest boy. A moment later, the little boy ran up to Doggie and yanked Doggie's ears. Hard.

For a second it seemed he was going to leave Doggie alone. But the other older boy shouted to him. The youngest boy turned back and grabbed Doggie's hind legs. He ripped Doggie from the lamppost so fast that Doggie's head jerked right under the ribbon. The ribbon was left behind, still tied around the lamppost. Then the boy hurled Doggie away.

The boys all ran off. The older two laughed and kicked their football back and forth. The youngest followed, trying to catch up.

Sat on the sofa, Anne shook her head and leant back. Lily and Pilot snuggled up beside her. "Doggie was bullied," she said as she stroked them. "That should never happen. Not to children or grown-ups or animals or toys."

Lily and Pilot looked at Anne, listening.

"Bullying," Anne told them, "is not kind. People make fun of others or take things or chase them or frighten them. All to show off or to make themselves feel better; more important, more powerful. Or sometimes just because they think it's funny. Well, it isn't funny. It isn't funny at all."

Lily and Pilot got off the couch to rummage in their toy box. When they came back, tails wagging, they had each brought a toy for Anne. Playing tug-a-toy always made her feel better.

But not this time. Anne didn't feel like playing.

"Bullies are always brave when they think they won't get caught. But when they're caught, it turns out they aren't very brave at all," she told her girls.

She got off the couch, walked to the window and looked over at Doggie.

"I wish you could hear me," she said.

Doggie could hear her. Anne just didn't know it.

"But I'll tell you anyway. I know that boy. I'm going to find out why he bullied you. I'll make everything alright. I promise."

Anne pulled the curtains closed, and went upstairs to watch the ten o'clock news in bed. The newsreaders talked about bullying in schools and workplaces.

"Not just in schools and workplaces," Anne told them. "On lampposts, too!"

She got up and looked down on Doggie from her bedroom window.

He was still there, in a halo of silver light that shone from the lamp above. Not a soul was around. All was quiet and calm.

Bullies need to be stopped, Anne thought. She was determined as she got back into bed.

By the time she fell asleep, Anne had decided what she needed to do to make sure Doggie wasn't bullied again. Sometimes, bullies just need a little help to learn what is right.

Chapter 5

The Bully

Anne had promised Doggie she'd make everything right. But she knew stopping a bully was not always easy. Sometimes the hardest part was telling someone that it was happening. Luckily, Anne had found out on her own.

What should I do? Anne had thought as she tried to sleep.

Should she make sure the bully is told off? Might that make the bullying worse? Tell the bully to be nice? But would a bully listen to that? Use a magic spell to change the bully?

"With a wave of my wand
I am casting this spell!
You will bully no more!
You will now behave well!
DULCIS ES! STATIM!"

Except Anne didn't believe in magic spells. And a bully wouldn't magically change.

In the end, Anne had decided she would go to the bully's house. She would tell his parents. Nothing scares a bully more than that.

She took Doggie with her. She untied him from the lamppost and fixed the purple ribbon like a school tie to make him really smart.

"There." She smiled. "You look amazing. Now, I'm taking you on an adventure!"

She placed Doggie at the bottom of her handbag so he wouldn't fall out.

"I'm amazing!" Doggie giggled as he wriggled back up to the top of Anne's handbag, climbing past tissues and perfume and lipstick and a comb, and the rest of the strange stuff ladies carry. He wanted to pop his head out to see what an adventure looked like.

Their adventure took them to the very expensive door of a very big house.

Anne rang the bell.

"Mrs Fairchild," said the man who opened the door. "You haven't found Jack's daft cat locked in your garage again, have you?"

"No, Mr Smith." Anne smiled. "I have something I'd like to show you. Have you got a moment?"

He hesitated, wondering how

long this might take. He was planning on taking his son, Jack, for a kickabout. "Okay, come on in."

"Thank you," said Anne. She sat down in the living room. Mrs Smith came downstairs.

"Hello, Mrs Fairchild." She smiled. "I'm glad you're here – I've been meaning to tell you that we're picking up a tracker collar for Chloe tomorrow. Now we'll know which garage she's got herself locked into when she goes missing! Jack gets so upset when she's gone."

"That's good news about Chloe's collar. Actually, I've come to see you about Jack," Anne told them.

"Oh?" said Mrs Smith.

"About a toy I found under my hedge," Anne began. She started to rummage in her handbag for Doggie and was surprised to find him right at the top. She showed him to Jack's parents.

"I doubt he'd have anything to do with this. He's always holed up in his bedroom building aeroplanes to hang from his ceiling," Mr Smith said.

"May I please speak to him anyway?" Anne asked, cradling Doggie on her lap.

"Alright," agreed Mrs Smith. She went upstairs to get Jack.

While she was gone, Mr Smith continued grumbling. "Aeroplanes! He should be out, kicking around a football!"

Mrs Smith came back downstairs. Jack bounded into the living room behind her.

Suddenly, he froze. Right there on Anne's lap was the doggie from the lamppost. He gulped. Oh, no ... Did she know what he'd done? Had she come to tell his parents? He sat nervously beside his mum.

Doggie had seen Jack, too. Wide-eyed and shaking,

he snuggled into Anne for protection. He wasn't sure he liked this adventure any more!

"Hello, Jack," Anne said. Then she told them the whole story. She began with how Lily had found Doggie and ended with how she had found Doggie lying on the grass.

"That's awful." Mrs Smith frowned.

"Doggie was too far away from the lamppost for him to have just fallen," Anne said. "And the ribbon I used to tie him to it was still there with its bow done up."

"How strange. But what does this have to do with Jack?" Mrs Smith asked.

"I'll show you," said Anne.

She put Doggie back into her handbag and took out her mobile phone. Doggie gave Jack a worried glance before scurrying to the bottom to be safe.

Anne showed them the CCTV clip.

Jack's mum and dad were shocked.

"Son!" exclaimed Mr Smith, his eyes glued to the mobile's screen. "That's you!"

"Jack!" Mrs Smith gasped. "Why did you do that?"

Jack didn't answer.

He was gone.

Chapter 6

The Victims

Jack had fled upstairs. They heard his bedroom door slam.

"Will you please excuse me?" Mrs Smith asked, smiling at Anne through her shock. She hurried upstairs.

She knocked on his door. "Jack, come down and explain yourself!"

"No," Jack called through the door. "I'm changing."

"Changing? What for?" His mum opened the door.

Jack really was changing. He was putting on the football shirt his dad had bought him for the new football season.

Downstairs, Anne waited with Mr Smith who was fuming. "He'll get a red card for this!"

Anne didn't think that would help, but she didn't say anything.

It was a good few minutes before Jack came back into the living room with his mum. He didn't look at them.

Mr Smith stood up. "Well, son," he began, "that was shocking. What do you have to say for yourself?"

Tears welled up in Jack's eyes as he blurted out, "They made me do it!"

"You mean those boys in the video?" Mrs Smith asked, her forehead creased.

Jack nodded and sniffed. "They don't go to my school. They're always in the park or on the street playing football. Yesterday, they asked if I wanted to play." He hesitated. "I said okay."

"You did?" said Mrs Smith. Anne noticed her eyebrows shoot up.

Jack looked at his mum, then at his dad. "They said I could play if I proved I was cool."

"Cool?" asked Mrs Smith. "And how were you supposed to prove that?"

Jack couldn't look at them. "They told me to bash the toy, tear it off the lamppost and throw it away," he admitted softly.

He looked up at his dad and mum with pleading eyes. "I didn't want to. But they made me." He burst into tears. "They didn't even let me play!"

"I didn't think football was that important to you," Mrs Smith said.

Jack quietly admitted, "It's not. I'm sorry, Dad, but I really don't like football."

Mr Smith looked hard at Jack. "You don't? But you're wearing your new shirt!"

Jack looked at his dad. "I put it on for you. I know

you want me to like football. That's why I was trying to play with those boys. I wanted you to be proud of me. But I like aeroplanes. I want to be a pilot, not a footballer."

Mr Smith's eyes grew wide and his eyebrows lifted. He fell back into his chair with a huge sigh. He didn't know what to say or do.

But Mrs Smith did. She gave Jack a hug.

"Sweetheart," she said softly, "we'll be proud of you whatever you want to be."

Mr Smith got up and put his arms around his family.

"Your mum's right," he said. "We love you just for you."

Jack looked up at his dad. "I didn't want to disappoint you."

"I'm not too disappointed you don't want to be a footballer," said Mr Smith. "But I am disappointed in you for what you did in that video. No matter the reason, you shouldn't have done it. Do you have something to say about that?"

Everyone was quiet for a moment as Jack went to Anne.

"Mrs Fairchild, I'm really sorry for what I did."

"Thank you, Jack." Anne smiled.

"May I please see the toy dog for a minute? To check he's okay?" Jack asked, hopefully.

"No! No! No! No! No!" cried Doggie from the bottom of Anne's handbag. But Anne couldn't hear him.

"Of course," Anne replied. "I'm calling him Doggie until his owner turns up."

She found Doggie at the bottom of her handbag, fished him out and handed him to Jack.

28

Doggie scrunched his eyes closed. When he felt kind hands around his middle, holding him gently, he peeked at Jack out of one eye. Jack didn't look scary now.

"It's clear you didn't really want to pull Doggie down. You were bullied, too, by those boys," Anne told Jack. "Don't let people like them stop you from being the decent, caring person I believe you really are. You're better than those bullies," Anne added. "And good luck becoming a pilot. My husband was a pilot – an airline captain. He had model aeroplanes, too, when he was your age."

Then Mr Smith said, "Son, I'd like to help you build your models."

Jack smiled. "That would be great!" He handed Doggie back to Anne. "Thank you for being so nice, Mrs Fairchild."

As the very expensive door closed behind them, Anne whispered to Doggie, now happily watching from her handbag, "What an adventure we've had! Jack is really a lovely lad."

Chapter 7

Finding Thinks and Memories

Anne was so happy walking home from the Smiths' that she sang softly to herself.

Doggie listened as he looked over the top of her handbag. Her song filled him with glee. He began to hum along. He had never sung before so his tune was a little wobbly. But that was okay. His voice was only little so no one heard him. He was just having fun. He'd never been this happy.

Anne stopped at the lamppost. Taking him from her handbag, she gave him a cuddle. "I wish I didn't have to put you back on the lamppost," she whispered in his ear as she tied him there with the purple ribbon. She made a lovely bow behind him. "But it wouldn't be right not to. Your owner might come for you today."

Doggie was so happy that he didn't mind watching as Anne, Lily and Pilot left for their walk. And he didn't even mind being back on the lamppost, especially when people who passed by stopped to tell him kind things like: "You're lovely," "You're so cute," and "I bet you've seen a lot from up there!"

What he saw now made him wriggle with even more happiness. Jack and his parents were coming.

"Hello, Doggie." Jack smiled when he got close. "I have a nice surprise for you. Close your eyes."

Doggie did as he was told. He felt Jack tickle his ears.

"There you go." Jack grinned. "You can open your eyes now."

Doggie saw a smile, and kindness shining in Jack's eyes. He blinked and smiled back.

Just then, Anne returned from her walk with Lily and Pilot.

"Hello," she said, joining them.

"Hello," they said back.

Jack beamed. "I've finished," he told them.

"Finished?" Anne smiled. "Finished what?"

Jack replied shyly, "We went shopping 'cause there was something I wanted to get Doggie to make it up to him after what I did. Are they okay, Mrs Fairchild?"

Anne looked at Doggie. There were ribbons around his ears. Purple, to match the ribbon tying him to the lamppost.

"They're splendid. That's really thoughtful, Jack," Anne told him.

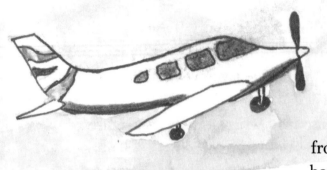

"Doggie's day just keeps getting better."

"So does ours." Mr Smith smiled, showing her a bag from a toy shop. "We bought –"

"– a Piper Warrior!" Jack finished for him. "Dad's going to help me make it."

"I am." Mr Smith nodded. "We'd better get home so you can tell me what we need to do."

Jack gave Doggie a quick cuddle and patted Lily and Pilot. Then the Smiths left. Jack chattered excitedly with his dad about the model plane.

"Time for us to go, too, Doggie." Anne sighed. "See you soon."

Doggie grinned as he watched them all go inside. Then he called out, as loudly as he could, "Lily! Pilot!"

A moment later, he saw the girls dash to the living room window to look over at him.

"Doggie, what is it?" Lily asked, alarmed.

"I've had a think!" Doggie called to them, wriggling about under the ribbon and almost bursting with happiness. "The fluff in my head has thinks with marvellous memories in them."

Lily and Pilot barked and wagged their tails, so excited for him.

Doggie was even more excited. He couldn't stop talking. "I think you both really like me. So does your mummy. And Jack. And the people who talked to me when they passed the lamppost today. I think the animals who visit me every night

32

are all my friends, too." Doggie's eyes shone in amazement. "How come I can find thinks with memories now?"

Lily's tail kept thumping as she spoke. "It must be because you feel cared about, and that makes wonderful things happen, like the fluff in your head giving you thinks and memories."

But Doggie still had no thinks with any memories in his fluff from before Lily found him under the hedge.

He suddenly felt confused. Did he really want his owner to find him and take him away? He wasn't sure any more.

Visit Hubble and Hattie on the web:
www.hubbleandhattie.com • www.hubbleandhattie.blogspot.co.uk
Details of all books • Special offers • Newsletter • New book news

33

Chapter 8

"Lily, How Come You Can Read?"

On his third day tied to the lamppost, Doggie was happy because now he had thinks with marvellous memories in the fluff in his head. But he had no thinks or memories about his owner ...

Anne was the one having all the thinks about Doggie's owner. She was wondering what else she could do to get Doggie found.

She'd already put him on the lamppost for his owner to see him. She'd already posted him on Lost It? Find It! She'd already put up signs about him everywhere.

The problem was Doggie was still waiting on the lamppost.

"There's always more than one way to solve a problem," Anne had to remind herself. She wrote a notice about Doggie and stuck it to the lamppost above his head.

Lily watched Anne drive away to meet friends for tea.

Then she called out to Doggie. "Mummy just put a notice up for your owner. Shall I try and read it to you?"

"Oh, yes, please," answered Doggie.

"Well, it says something about teatime two days from now, and something about a bubble bath."

"Oooh." Doggie smiled. "Teatime sounds yummy, but what's a bubble bath?"

"I don't know," Lily admitted. "But it sounds like fun."

"And an adventure!" Doggie jiggled with joy.

Then a think came out of his fluff in the shape of a question.

"Lily, how come you can read?"

"Pilot can read, too," Lily told him. "But only a little. It's because we go to school every week with Mummy where children read to us. Sometimes they sound out the letters before saying the word."

"Letters?" Doggie asked, crinkling his brow.

"They're squiggles on paper," Lily answered, "with names like A, B and C. Letters are magical because when you read them they make different sounds. There are loads of them in the alphabet."

"In the what?" Doggie asked.

"The alphabet. It's like a house where all the

letters live," Lily told him.

Doggie wrinkled his brow. He was curious. "How many letters are there?"

"Twenty-six," Lily answered.

Doggie's eyes grew wide in amazement. "What a lot of letters! It must be a very noisy house."

"No, it's quiet," Lily told him. "They just sleep there until they have to join up with other letters to make words."

"How do they do that?" Doggie asked, fascinated.

"They just put their sounds together. Like when the letters D, O and G join to make the word DOG. Putting together lots of letters and words is how you make a story. Children read really good stories to Pilot and me at school. Our favourite is *Simon Super-Paws: 009, Secret Agent*. Simon has great adventures."

Doggie's eyes lit up. "I love adventures!"

"The children sometimes pet us

while they read to us," Lily went on. "And they give us treats after they read, too."

Children reading to dogs sounded wonderful. Doggie started wishing he could go to school with Lily so children could read books to them together, especially *Simon Super-Paws: 009, Secret Agent.*

There was so much to look forward to that he stopped hoping his owner would find him soon. He even stopped hoping that his owner would find him at all!

Visit Hubble and Hattie on the web:
www.hubbleandhattie.com • www.hubbleandhattie.blogspot.co.uk
Details of all books • Special offers • Newsletter • New book news

Chapter 9

Hello and Goodbye

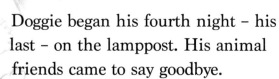

Doggie began his fourth night – his last – on the lamppost. His animal friends came to say goodbye.

Honey, the doe, with Trek, her fawn, stepped daintily into the silvery halo of the street light.

"Hello," she said.

"Hi," Doggie replied. He watched Trek follow confidently on thin legs.

"He doesn't wobble at all now, does he?" Honey said proudly. "He'll be a fine young buck, I think. We must go, Doggie. We just wanted to wish you great happiness."

Honey leaned over and kissed

38

Doggie. He had never been kissed before. Her kiss made him feel very special indeed!

She smiled at him. "Goodbye." She nuzzled Trek. "Come along, precious."

Honey and Trek stepped out of the light. With a flick of their tails, they were gone into the woods.

Next, Chloe, Jack's cat, padded by.

She stretched her front paws up the lamppost. "Look Doggie, I have a special collar now. It's got a tracker. Now if I get locked in a garage, my family can find me. They worry when they think I'm lost." Then she remembered why Doggie was still on the lamppost. "I shouldn't have said that." She meowed. "I know your owner hasn't found you yet. I'm sure you'll be found soon."

Doggie hoped not. His thinks were happier than they'd ever been. Already they were turning into dreams. One dream was to go to school with Lily and have a child read *Simon Super-Paws: 009, Secret Agent* to them.

"Chloe, do you know Simon Super-Paws?" he asked.

Chloe's eyes brightened. "I wish I did. Can you imagine if he were real?" she said. "Everyone loves him. He's the best cat spy ever! I have to go now, Doggie. Goodbye, and good luck!" She purred as she wandered slowly down the street, dreaming about Simon.

Doggie was just drifting into sleep when the foxes woke him.

"Hi, Doggie," Vixie yelped, jumping into the silver light and looking up at him. "We're not slinking on our tummies or

sneaking across the road tonight. Know why?"

Doggie shook his head.

"Because," whispered Alf, "we've finished our secret mission."

"Secret mission?" asked Doggie.

Vixie checked around her before admitting, "We're secret agents. But don't tell."

Doggie's eyes grew wide. "Like Simon Super-Paws?" he asked.

"Kind of." Alf smiled. "We know Chloe told you about him."

"You do?" asked Doggie, his eyes widening in amazement.

"It's our job to know. We're secret agents, remember?" Vixie said.

"Chloe's right about Simon. He really is the best agent ever." Alf nodded.

"Chloe and her friends think he's only make-believe. If they knew he was real, they'd yowl like crazy!" Vixie said.

"This is our last night here, too, Doggie," Alf said. "We've been promoted to Buckingham Palace. If you're ever there, come and see us."

"Bye and good luck," whispered Vixie.

Then, being secret agents, they vanished into the shadows.

Doggie's thinks were so full of Vixie and Alf and

Buckingham Palace that he was startled when the bats and owls swooped around him.

The bats zoomed every which way, squeaking and clicking. Then they were gone.

Ombra, the owl, landed near the lamppost. She hooted. "The bats wish you good luck."

"They almost hit me!" Doggie cried.

"No, they didn't," she assured him. "Their squeaks and clicks bounce off your lamppost so they know where it is and can fly around it."

Doggie frowned. "Really?"

"Really. There's no time to explain more," Ombra said. "It's almost dawn and we must fly to our nests. Good luck, Doggie. We hope you find a name soon. Goodbye." And away the owls went.

The street light had gone off and the sun was almost up when Mrs Pinny, the hedgehog, shuffled to the lamppost with her four little hoglets.

"Doggie!" she grunted, very upset. "We've come to say goodbye. I thought we weren't going to make it at all because our house was squashed to make room for human houses. I barely escaped with my babies!" Mrs Pinny wiped her eyes and snuffled. "I don't know where we will live now."

"I wish I could help you," Doggie said. "Everyone needs a good home."

"That's very kind,

Doggie," she replied. "You need a home, too, though. Don't you worry about us. Good luck, Doggie. Bye." She tearfully waddled off, her four little ones trailing behind.

As the sun rose, Doggie knew he'd had lots of happy thinks. But one think was unhappy and much larger than the others. It was about Mrs Pinny and her babies. How could he help them? He was going to need a very special think for that.

Chapter 10

Off the Lamppost

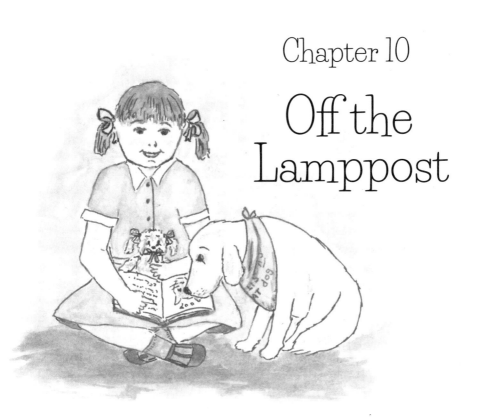

Doggie was trying to have a very special think about how to help Mrs Pinny and her hoglets. Their home had been squashed, and he wondered where they would live now. Then he wondered where *he* would live now. He knew this was his last day on the lamppost.

As the sun's rays warmed him, his thinks warmed him, too. He was happier than he had ever been. Love and kindness had changed the fluff in his head in wonderful ways. He had thrilling thinks and marvellous memories now. But still none from before he was under the hedge. He knew now that he didn't want to be found by his owner.

When teatime came and went with no sign of Doggie's owner, Anne went to the lamppost. She smiled. "Let's go inside, Doggie. Lily and Pilot are waiting for you." She untied the purple ribbon and held him gently.

Then, a family came by.

"Look! The doggie's off the lamppost," the little girl said.

"Hello," said Anne, smiling at them. "Is this your doggie?"

"Oh, no," the mother answered. "But we've been seeing him there for days."

"Please may I hold him?" the little girl asked, shyly.

Anne gave her Doggie, and the girl stroked his head.

"I'm Sophia. I'm five," she told Doggie, holding up five fingers to show him. "I like your ribbons."

She looked at her parents. "Please may Doggie come to our house for tea?"

Everyone thought that was a lovely idea, especially Doggie. Another fun adventure!

After the family left, Anne whispered, "I was afraid that was your owner. Let's hurry inside before anyone else comes."

Lily and Pilot jumped about with floppy ears and wagging tails, excited to have Doggie in the house again.

"Now, Doggie, time for your bubble bath." Anne smiled.

She sat Doggie on the kitchen counter. Wide-eyed and smiling, he watched the bubbles get bigger and bigger.

"I've got you little yellow ducks to play with," Anne said as she picked him up from the counter. Doggie's feet were dangling right above the bubbles when the doorbell rang.

"Now who's that?" Anne wondered. She sat Doggie back on the worktop beside the sink. His shoulders slumped while he waited.

Anne opened the door to a lady she didn't know.

"Hello," the lady began. "May I ask, did you just take a doggie off that lamppost?"

"Yes, I did." Anne nodded.

The lady hesitated then said, "My little boy here, Eddie, would like to see him." Eddie peeked out from behind his mother. "Would that be okay?"

"Of course," Anne replied with a small smile. *Oh, dear,* she thought. Was this Doggie's owner? "I'll just get him."

Anne went to the kitchen and picked him up. As they went to the front door, she whispered, "Your owner might be here."

Oh, no! Doggie's think was loud. He quivered as Anne handed him to the little boy.

"Thank you so much," the lady said.

"Thank you," Eddie said, very politely, and gave Doggie a huge cuddle.

"Eddie has big plans for this doggie," the boy's mum told Anne.

Oh, dear, she thought again. *He's planning on taking Doggie home.* Then, to Anne's surprise, Eddie handed Doggie back to her.

"Eddie would like to take him on a teddy bear hunt for his third birthday next Saturday," the lady said. "Would you like to bring the doggie and stay for tea?"

"That would be lovely." Anne smiled. Doggie

jiggled in delight –
another adventure!

"Thank you," the lady
said. "You've made Eddie's
day."

As they left, Anne told
Doggie, "I'm glad that
wasn't your owner. Now,
ready for your bubble bath?"

The water was warm. The bubbles were big. So big that
Anne even made Doggie a bubble hat. The mummy duck
and her ducklings quacked softly to him. Afterwards, when
he was clean and fluffy, Anne tied new blue ribbons in bows
around his neck and ears, and told him how handsome he
was. His thrilling thinks were overflowing.

Three days later, Anne told him, "It's time for another
adventure. You're coming to school with Lily and me."

Though Anne wanted to keep Doggie, she felt she should
try one last time to find his owner.

So Doggie found himself at morning assembly. The
headteacher, Mr Bentley, held him and introduced him to
all the children.

"Doggie's a cute little chap," Mr Bentley told the children.
"But does anyone know who he belongs to? If you do, please
tell us so he can go home."

After assembly, Doggie's wish came true when a little girl
snuggled him onto her lap and read *Simon Super-Paws: 009,
Secret Agent* to him and Lily.

Chapter 11

The Star of the School

The children loved having Doggie at school. He went to listen to them read every Thursday with Lily, and every Friday with Pilot.

At the next governors' meeting, Anne introduced Doggie. The governors decided to have a woodland nature study in the playground. Anne was put in charge.

When the meeting ended, Anne popped Doggie into her handbag and headed home.

Doggie wriggled up to poke his head out so he could see where they were going. He heard Anne mutter, "A woodland nature study ... now, what should go in it?"

Doggie knew. "I kept telling your mummy my think on the way back, but she never heard me," he told Lily and Pilot that night. He had already told them about Mrs Pinny and her hoglets and their squashed house. "If Mrs Pinny and her hoglets could move into a hedgehog house in the school's woodland nature study, they'd have somewhere safe to live!"

Lily and Pilot agreed that was a brilliant idea. And Lily knew exactly how to tell Anne. After Anne went to bed, Lily opened Anne's laptop and got to work.

When Anne opened her laptop in the morning, her eyebrows shot up in amazement. "What's going on?" The entire screen was filled with hedgehog houses. "How did all these pictures get here?" Anne said, before deciding it didn't matter. "A hedgehog house would be perfect for the woodland nature study."

That morning, at school with Lily and Doggie, she told Mr Bentley.

"A hedgehog house?" he asked. "Remember our budget. What will it cost?"

"Nothing." Anne smiled. "I have a plan. Doggie's here a lot. The children love him. But 'Doggie' is *what* he is, not *who* he is. The children could suggest names for him and pay 10p for every suggestion. Then they could vote to choose his name. Doggie will get a name, the school will get a hedgehog house, and Doggie and the children will get the credit."

"Splendid!" Mr Bentley grinned. "Go ahead then. I'll send a note home with the children today."

Continued on page 57

48

Doggie is found
under a hedge.

Doggie is tied onto the
nearest lamppost with a
purple ribbon.

Sophia invited Doggie to
a tea party to meet other
toys.

Eddie and Doggie had fun on their teddy bear hunt.

Doggie relaxes in the warm bubble bath with three ducklings.

50

Lily looks concerned. "Doggie is all wet! May I lick him dry?"

When Doggie is dry, he gets ribbons and sits in the sun on a bench at the local shopping centre.

Veterinary surgeon Lucy Atkinson, assisted by student veterinary nurse Ashleigh Sawyer, gives Doggie a physical examination, first listening to his heart ...

... then checking his ears ...

... and his eyes.

Dr Lucy and student nurse Ashleigh, with Lily beside Lucy, Doggie in the middle, and Pilot beside Ashleigh.

Jasmine reads to Doggie and Lily in Read2Dogs.

School children
(left to right) Maddie,
Ellie, Jackson, Charles
and Ebony, showing their
new hegdehog house and
insect hotel, with their
headteacher, Doggie, Pilot
and Lily.

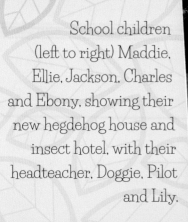

"Mrs Pinny, are you
home?" called Doggie,
visiting her new house for
the first time.

Clare, the school librarian,
helps Doggie check out the
insect-friendly hotel.

Doggie revisits where he was found, and recalls his amazing journey from the hedge to Buckingham Palace, and a forever family.

Lily and Pilot, wearing their Pets As Therapy bandanas.

Doggie with Lily.

Doggie with Lily and Laura.

Doggie with his forever family: Pilot, Lily and Laura.

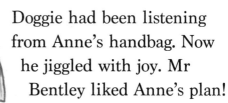

Doggie had been listening from Anne's handbag. Now he jiggled with joy. Mr Bentley liked Anne's plan! Mrs Pinny and her babies might soon have a house, and he might soon have a name.

At school the next morning, children brought money in, excitedly telling their teachers their names for Doggie. In only a few days, the children suggested so many names that the teachers had to sharpen all their pencils to write them down. They had to get more paper to write the names on, too. And they collected so much money the school nearly needed another bank account.

At morning assembly two weeks later, Mr Bentley thanked the children and said, "Mrs Fairchild will pick three names for Doggie, and then we'll vote."

"Yeah!" the children cheered.

"Doggie has raised a lot of money," Mr Bentley continued. "We have been able to buy a hedgehog house and a friendly insect hotel and even a night vision CCTV camera so we can see what happens at night and help to keep the hedgehogs safe. In fact, Doggie has raised so much money that we can give a hedgehog house, a friendly insect hotel and a night vision CCTV camera to three other schools! So, thank you, Doggie! And thank you, children!"

"Yeah for Doggie!" the children cheered again.

"I have another surprise for you," Mr Bentley added. "Tomorrow a television crew, newspaper reporters and photographers will be coming to see us put it all in our woodland nature study."

"Yeah!" the children cheered. "We're going to be on TV!"

The next day, excited reporters scrambled to hear Doggie's story. Because of him, hedgehogs would have a home. Friendly insects would have a hotel. The children would be able to see the woodland at night.

'Abandoned under a hedge, lost doggie finds fame!' was a headline on the news at six o'clock and ten o'clock. The front page of the papers read 'Doggie rescued by a doggie' and 'Doggie saves hedgehog family.'

But Doggie's story wasn't over yet. Everyone was eager to know what his name would be. No one was more eager than Doggie, Lily, Pilot and Anne. Anne had a very long list of names to look through. Which would be Doggie's?

Chapter 12
Who Will Doggie Be?

At home, Anne began reading all the names suggested for Doggie. They went on for pages!

She thought she was choosing the new name for Doggie, but really, with Lily's help, Doggie was choosing it for himself. At each name he liked he asked Lily to woof. Anne took Lily's woofs as a sign, and put a tick by those names.

The problem was that Doggie wanted a name so badly that Lily had to woof at every name Anne read.

When Anne came to 'Sophia,' Doggie wriggled about in excitement.

"Lily, woof! I really want to be 'Sophia.' Sophia invited me to her tea party!" Doggie said.

So Lily woofed.

"'Sophia?'" Anne asked. "Are you woofing for a girl's name, Lily?"

Lily was, so she woofed again.

Anne shrugged her shoulders. "Alright." She ticked 'Sophia,' then continued reading: 'Lucky,' 'Hope,' 'Dazzle,' even 'Furry MacFur-Face.' Doggie wanted them all.

But when Anne read 'Eddie,' he wriggled about in excitement again.

"Lily, woof! I want to be 'Eddie!' He's taking me on a teddy bear hunt! On another adventure!"

So Lily woofed, and Anne ticked 'Eddie.'

On and on it went until it was nearly bedtime. Anne read the last name, "'HRH Prince George.'"

Doggie wriggled more than he had ever wriggled before. "Lily, woof! I *really* want to be 'HRH Prince George.'"

But Lily wouldn't woof. She told him, "HRH means His Royal Highness. You're not royal. Not a highness. Not a prince. So you can't be 'HRH Prince George.'"

Doggie slumped and hung his head. Then he straightened and brightly told Lily, "I'll just be 'George' then. Lily, woof! Woof!"

So Lily woofed. She had hardly any woofs left.

The next morning, Doggie went to school with Anne, Lily and Pilot. Reporters, photographers and TV crews were there again, asking "What will Doggie's new name be?"

The children sat in lines on the hall floor for assembly. At the front with Mr Bentley were Doggie, Anne, Lily and Pilot. Doggie felt special. Everyone was there just for him.

Mr Bentley smiled. "Children, today we have to welcome our guests from TV, newspapers and radio, here to learn what Doggie's new name will be and to hear about our woodland nature study. Our camera has already caught a mummy hedgehog with four hoglets in our hedgehog house!"

The children clapped and cheered, "Yeah!"

So did Doggie. He knew Mrs Pinny and her hoglets were safe in their new home!

"Now," Mr Bentley continued, "let's choose Doggie's name. Mrs Fairchild has –"

He stopped when Miss Brisk, the secretary, bustled up in an important hurry. She whispered to him. His mouth fell open. He whispered to Anne. Her mouth fell open, too.

At once, Mr Bentley turned to the deputy head. "Miss Jones, take the assembly! Mrs Fairchild and I must leave!"

They rushed out of the hall, with Miss Brisk hurrying behind them.

The children began whispering to each other as Miss Jones tried to continue the assembly.

It was five minutes before Mr Bentley and Anne came back into the hall. Miss Jones stepped aside.

"Children and guests," Mr Bentley began, almost too excited to speak. "I have something amazing to tell you. Mrs

Fairchild and I just had to take a very important phone call about Doggie. Because of him, hedgehogs can live in safety, and friendly insects can have lives that matter. Doggie will be rewarded for that today at –"

Mr Bentley paused. Everyone leaned forward to hear.

"– Buckingham Palace!"

"Ooooh!" Everyone clapped and cheered. The photographers were so surprised they almost dropped their cameras.

Mr Bentley smiled. "This morning, His Royal Highness Prince George will give Doggie an award! A helicopter is coming any moment to take him there with Mrs Fairchild, Lily, Pilot and me."

Everyone clapped and cheered louder than ever.

"We must vote on Doggie's name right away. Mrs Fairchild has chosen three of the names for Doggie. 'George,' 'Sophia' and 'Eddie.' We'll start with 'George.' Raise your hand if you think Doggie's name should be 'George.'"

Every single person raised their hand. Even the reporters, photographers and camera crews did.

"Doggie." Mr Bentley laughed. "Everyone wants your name to be 'George' – just like Prince George!"

That very moment there was a chop-chop-chop-chop outside. Everything started to shake. Even the air in the hall started to shake. Excited chatter rose from the children and filled the hall.

Mr Bentley shouted above the throbbing noise of the helicopter, "Miss Jones, finish the assembly! The helicopter's here! We must go! We're flying to Buckingham Palace!"

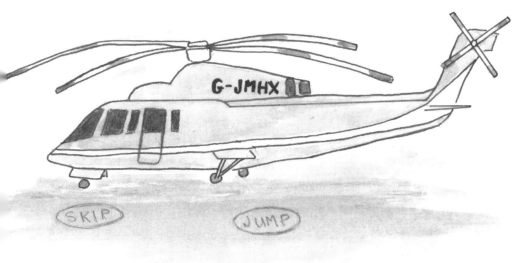

Visit Hubble and Hattie on the web:
www.hubbleandhattie.com • www.hubbleandhattie.blogspot.co.uk
Details of all books • Special offers • Newsletter • New book news

Chapter 13
Doggie's Diary

You'll never guess where I was today! Buckingham Palace!

What a great way to start my first diary. It was Lily's idea. She's writing it all down for me so I can remember this special day forever.

One minute Mr Bentley was telling the children to vote on a name for me right away, because a helicopter was coming to take us to Buckingham Palace. The next minute he announced everyone wanted my name to be 'George!' Then the helicopter landed in the playground making everything shake, even the air.

"Quick, Mrs Fairchild!" Mr Bentley had shouted over the chop-chop-chop of the helicopter. "The helicopter's waiting! Come on, Lily, Pilot!"

We all clambered aboard. I watched from the top of Mummy's handbag as we whizzed above the school and the trees and the houses. Soon we were over London. Before long we saw Buckingham Palace. We landed right outside.

Royal servants took us to the ballroom and showed us to our seats in the front row. They were all labelled with our names. Mr Bentley had a chair, then there were comfy red cushions for Pilot and Lily.

Beside Lily was a chair for 'Mrs Fairchild,' and beside her was my chair with my brand new name on it: George!

Suddenly, I heard a "Pssst!" right next to me. I looked around but I couldn't see anyone I knew.

"Pssst!" I heard it again.

Then someone nearby lifted their dark glasses and whispered, "It's me! Alf!"

"Alf!" I laughed.

"I'm here, too," someone else whispered, lifting the brim of their big hat. It was Vixie!

The foxes were disguised so fantastically that I hadn't recognised them at all. They told me they'd asked for this secret agent duty especially to see me get my award.

Vixie leaned so close I was under the brim of her hat. Her whiskers tickled. She said, "Simon Super-Paws wants you to know he was at school to

watch the vote for your name. He radioed the Palace to change the sign on your chair to 'George' before sneaking into your helicopter. He'd hoped to see you receive your award, but was ordered to Downing Street."

I wanted to ask what Downing Street was but she and Alf had already vanished. Everyone stood up suddenly. The Queen was coming in, with Prince George behind her. Musicians played *God Save The Queen*. Men bowed and ladies curtsied as they were given their awards.

Then it was Prince George's turn to give me my award.

"Hi, George!" He laughed and cuddled me.

He sat me on a gold cushion held by a servant and said, "I give you this award for helping hedgehogs and friendly insects to have homes and lives that matter!"

Prince George tied my award around my neck. It's a sparkly blue diamond collar with a little dog bone on it!

Afterwards, TV crews and reporters all crowded round me.

This evening, I was on the six o'clock news again, and I'm going be on the ten o'clock news again, too. But I'll probably miss it, because I can hardly keep my eyes open.

Before I fall asleep, though, I have to write down something else that happened. My very special human has just cuddled me. She told me they all love me and are going to take care of me.

"This is your home now, George," she said. "But you'll always be 'Doggie' to me," she whispered, giving me a kiss goodnight. I'm your mummy now, just like I am for Lily and Pilot."

How wonderful is that?

It really was fabulous seeing the Queen and Prince George, being in Buckingham Palace and getting my sparkly diamond award.

But what's better is being truly loved and finally having my forever home with Lily, Pilot and Mummy.

The Story Behind the Story

Lily – whose own inspiring story is told in *Lily: One in a Million, A Miracle of Survival* – and Pilot, her mother, are my Golden Retrievers. Both have been Pets As Therapy (PAT) dogs since they were nine months old, visiting residential care homes and schools as part of the Read2Dogs programme. As this book goes to print, their combined hours exceed 500, and their visits have been honoured by our borough council.

One day, when Lily and I were on our way to school, she really did rescue a lost toy dog from under my hedge; it inspired this story. I tried to notify the toy's owner by leaving the doggie tied to a lamppost where he would be seen. When social media, local signs and a notice failed to catch the attention of his owner I decided to keep Doggie and write this book about him.

As Doggie's story unfolds, love transforms him. The little lost doggie with only fluff and no thinks in his head becomes a celebrity doggie with thinks, memories and a forever family. He becomes more than he was ever manufactured to be, all because of love.

I hope you have enjoyed reading Doggie's book, especially now you know the story behind it.

Laura Hamilton

Acknowledgements

Marcus (my son), Elizabeth (my daughter) and Shaun (my son-in-law): you're my technological experts. Thank you for all your help.

Veterinary surgeon Lucy Atkinson and student veterinary nurse Ashleigh Sawyer: Lucy and Ashleigh, thank you both for your great sense of fun. The photos in this book show you examining Doggie and pronouncing him fit for his adventures with Lily.

Kathleen Curtis, my fabulous high-school English and Latin teacher in Ontario: Thank you, Kathleen, for your help after I wrote to you for advice about my Latin in Chapter 5's magic spell. You kindly reminded me to use the singular or the plural imperative. I've used the singular, but with so many bullies around, the plural is actually needed.

My neighbours Jacob, age 11, Logan, age 8, and Harry, age 5: Thank you for giving the story and the illustrations a 'test flight.' And for telling me everything about the book is super.

Kevin Atkins at Hubble & Hattie: just as you did for Lily's first book, you worked wonders, ensuring the photos enhance the story. When a picture is worth a thousand words, your expertise means a lot. Thank you very much.

Becky Taylor at Hubble & Hattie: your advice through your knowledge of children's publishing has helped enormously. In coming up with the perfect title, designing the cover, and presenting the book in its finished form, you have been marvellous. Thank you most sincerely for all you have done.

Jude Brooks, my publisher: Jude, you are a star. I'm so grateful for the fabulous opportunity you gave me to write this book, showing the transforming power of love. Your insight and compassion ensured the inclusion of the chapters on bullying and Pets As Therapy's Read2Dogs. I was thrilled you asked me to illustrate the book. Doing so was enormous fun. Thank you very, very much.

Also by Laura Hamilton ...

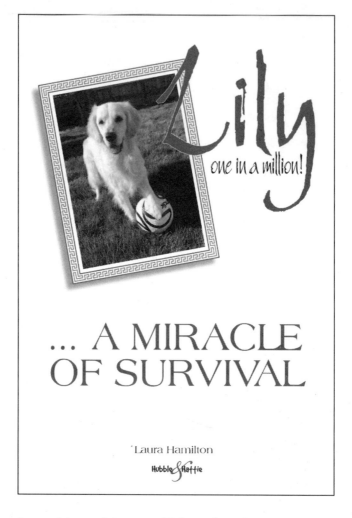

Lily
one in a million!

... A MIRACLE
OF SURVIVAL

Laura Hamilton

Hubble & Hattie

The moving and powerful story of Lily: a dog who was born unable to
survive unaided. But her owner's intensive, creative management of her rare
disability has given her a life worth living, and may inspire others not to give
up on animals with other life-threatening conditions. As a therapy dog, Lily
greatly enriches the lives of others.

ISBN: 978-1-787111-47-9
Paperback • 22.5x15.2cm • 72 pages • 38 pictures

Visit www.hubbleandhattie.com to find out more.